The Billionaire's Obsession

J.L. Ryan

Published by J.L. Ryan, 2024.

This is a work of fiction. Similarities to real people, places, or events are entirely coincidental.

THE BILLIONAIRE'S OBSESSION

First edition. May 26, 2024.

Copyright © 2024 J.L. Ryan.

ISBN: 979-8233400711

Written by J.L. Ryan.

The Billionaire's Obsession

The Country Club Disaster

 April's mind still reeled from the news. It was all anyone in her sorority house talked about, and all that she saw on the news. Lewis Edwards had been arrested and charged with securities fraud. It turned out that the investment scheme he was running truly was a scheme – a Ponzi scheme. He was bringing in new investors. Most of them were hardworking middle-class people looking to build retirement funds. It turned out that he was using their money to pay his high net worth investors. It all came crashing down on him, and in an attempt to pay back as much of the money as they could, the Feds seized all of Edwards' assets. The problem for April was that Lewis Edwards was her father. April would never have considered herself rich, but she was wealthy. They had enough money that she never worried about anything. She never even questioned why her mother left her father five years ago – though she suspected now that her mother got wise to his scheme and decided to leave. April felt bad now for insisting to stay with him. She had alienated her mother, and right now, she could have used a sympathetic shoulder to cry on. Everyone had abandoned her. Her boyfriend of two years broke up with her. Her friends turned their backs on her. April was alone and miserable.

 As the spring semester wrapped up, April somehow managed to make it through her finals and wondered what would happen next. Would she be able to come back to school? Would she even have a place to live? The home she had known her whole life was locked up and taped. It and everything inside was to be auctioned off this summer. April sat on the bed of her dorm room and looked out the window. Her roommate Sylvia had already left. Sylvia had hardly said a word to her since the news about her father came out. Of all of her friends, April thought Sylvia had the best reason. Her father had been one of the investors in the Edwards Fund, and he very likely lost a great deal of money. The day outside was bright, far brighter than April felt. She let out a long sigh. She had held off on calling her mother. She knew that her mother would not turn her away, but she was also not sure how she was going to get to her. She was across the country now, in California. While she had managed to pick up her life, April doubted that she would be able to spring for a plane ticket at the last minute. "You're still here," a light voice said from April's doorway. April turned to see her sorority sister Chloe standing there. She was holding a suitcase in one hand and a box under her other arm. "Yeah, I'm not in any hurry to get nowhere," April said.

Chloe set her things down at the doorway and walked over to Sylvia's old bed. She sat down and looked at April, measuring her carefully. April was not sure what to make of it. She and Chloe were never close. Chloe was a year her senior and a sweet girl, but the two of them had almost nothing in common. "It's been hard on you the last few weeks," Chloe said at last. "Do you know where you're going?" April shrugged her shoulders. "I'll probably call my mom out in California and see if I can join her out there." Chloe frowned. "That's a long way to go for an 'if you can.'" April appreciated Chloe's ability to quickly understand a situation; even she did not understand all of the details behind it. It did not help her though, and April let out another deep sigh before looking out the window again. "You know," Chloe said, "I might have a solution for you." April turned back to face Chloe. A solution was just what she needed. "What's that?" "My dad owns a resort upstate. He always needs extra help for the summer, and it pays really well. You also get to stay at the resort free, though you're staying in the servants' quarters. It's not too bad, as long as you don't mind spending your summer in a room about the size of this dorm room." April never had to work a summer job. She was aware of the concept, but the practice itself was alien to her. Still, the idea of getting a job had a certain appeal. It meant that she did not have to depend on her mother, and if her mother saw her trying to make an effort to get past everything and be better for it, it might help the two of them repair their relationship. If her mother could help, she might even be willing to do it on more even terms than April having to move somewhere strange. "Will it be a problem, to get me a job I mean?" April asked. Chloe shook her head. "My dad's opinion is that anyone who can't ask a few simple questions about an investment probably deserves to lose their money." Chloe paused and gave April an apologetic look. "It's a harsh opinion. But it means that he's not going to have anything against helping you. Besides, nothing that happened had anything to do with you. It was all your father." April gave Chloe the first real smile that she felt in weeks. "Thank you so much. Whatever he needs me to do, I don't care. I'll even wash toilets." Chloe laughed. "It won't be that bad. It'll be hard work, but the resort is beautiful, and staff always get two days off during the week, so you'll even get to enjoy some of it." April did not care about getting to enjoy the resort. For the first time since the investigation into her father started, April was starting to see the light at the end of a very dark tunnel. She even though it might not be a train.

April had never had the opportunity to visit Stuart Estates before. It was far more upscale than anything her family would have afforded, though she knew many of her father's clients probably frequented this resort. She wished she had gotten to see and enjoy it without having to be an employee. Set in a mountain valley, it featured a large manor house that hosted any number of events, from conferences to weddings and family reunions. Some of the upstairs rooms were still held as private rooms for guests, though a majority of guest accommodations were in "cabins," buildings that had once served as guest houses or were built later when the original property was converted. Still, April thought that she would enjoy working here. The air was crisp and clear. She was surrounded by beauty. It was tranquil, even if her supervisor Henry Graven did promise that she would be far too busy to take notice of what was around them. Mr. Graven was a cold man, tall with pale skin and dark hair. April recognized the name right away and did her best not to cringe. He was one of the people who lost their retirement money to her father's scheme. She could tell by the way that he looked at her; he knew who she was. He would not be able to do anything overt, but if she gave him any reason to fire her, he would not hesitate to take it.

An Inappropriate Encounter

Her first day was mostly a learning curve, of going from being the person waited on to doing the waiting. Mr. Graven was grudgingly patient as she learned, and she found the rest of the staff to be kind and understanding. She did not think any of them knew about her circumstances, and she was thankful for that. It was still a stressful day, and she was happy to retire in the evening to her room. Her "room" was one-half of a small cabin that April thought had probably been a campground cabin at some point. Now it was fitted with lighting and a small window unit to control heat and air. A bathroom had also been built onto it, to be shared between the two units. It was small, smaller than her dorm room had been, but it was comfortable, brightly decorated, and most of all private. April lay on her bed and thought about her day. It has been busy. Mr. Graven was right. She had barely had time to notice the beautiful scenery around her. She decided she would change that. She would give herself a few days to get used to the job, and after that, she would take brief moments in her day to just appreciate where she was.

April knelt down to wipe up the spilled coffee and gather up the shards of china cups that were now scattered about the floor. She was still getting used to carrying trays and keeping them balanced. Something had brushed her thigh over her skirt – it was not a something, it was a man's hand, she was certain of that – and caused her to lose her balance. Now, she was mortified as guests watched her fumbling with the glass shards and spilled coffee, trying hard not to cut herself. When the last piece was gathered and the last of the coffee sopped up, April stood, careful not to tip her tray and spill any of the shards. As she walked past a table, she felt a hand brush the top of her knee. She glanced back to see an older man with short, thick grey hair give her a wink. She quickly turned, trying to control her blush, and pushed through the swinging doors back into the kitchen galley. "Are you okay?" Leah, one of the other girls on staff asked her as she set down her tray of broken cups. "A guest is getting grabby," April said. She let out a sigh as she began to move the shards into the collection bin set up for broken wares. "It just caught me off guard, that's all." "You should be more careful with your tray Miss Edwards." Mr. Graven paused as he walked past her. "You are lucky that you did not burn anyone." "I'm sorry. I'll be more careful next time," April said. She did not look up to see Mr. Graven's look, but she was sure it was one of contempt. He walked on and she finished depositing the shards and took her tray to be washed. Another tray of coffee was set up, which Leah picked up to take out. April was relieved. She did not want to have to go back out into the dining room right now, not right on the heels of something so embarrassing.

The rest of the brunch went by smoothly, and when April did have to go back out, she was glad to see that guests paid her no more attention than they did to any other member of staff. Slowly the guests filed out of the dining hall and out to the veranda. It was still raining lightly outside, but it would clear soon. The guests would enjoy any number of outdoor festivities while the staff prepared the indoor rooms for evening festivities. April moved to her area of the dining room and began cleaning the tables. Someone else would come behind to vacuum, but she wanted to make sure that the floor was cleared of any large debris. As with everything else, she was still getting accustomed to cleaning, and the rest of the staff were done and cleared away as she still worked, her mind turning over bits of half-remembered lyrics to keep her moving at a steady pace. A hand moved over the small of April's back and along her buttock. She jumped up, pushing into the bulk of someone behind her. April had not even heard anyone come upon her. When she turned, she saw the same man with the grabby hands from brunch. "You're like a little rabbit." His voice was smooth as he spoke. His eyes were even and demanding. April gripped the table and tried to put space between them, only to have him close it again. "I do like hunting rabbits." "I need to finish my work." April could not think of anything else to say. The man's hands moved to her waist and slowly up her sides to cup her breasts. Everything happened at once then. The swinging door from the kitchen galley opened. Mr. Graven walked out, followed by two other staff members.

The door from the veranda opened and an older woman walked in, followed by two young men. April's hand collided with the face of the man accosting her with a loud slap propelled by the swing of her arm. It resounded through the dining hall before the woman began to scream shrilly. April tried to wrestle control of her situation, but she could not. Mr. Graven was upon the scene immediately, asking the man – Henry Worthington as it turned out to April's surprise and horror – if he were okay. The woman screamed about a trollop hitting her husband. Mr. Worthington began his explanation of how she had come onto him. April tried to speak up, to give her side of the story, only to be hushed by Mr. Graven or Mrs. Worthington screaming about lies. The noise brought more guests from the veranda into the dining room. Mr. Graven finally took hold of April's arm, squeezing tightly and leading her away. She tried to protest over his assurances to Mr. Worthington that he would take care of the situation. He led her out into the hall and spun her around hard, slamming her back against the wall and knocking the air from her. Further down, guests poured out of the dining room and into the hall, not wanting to miss the end of the drama. "I have been very patient with you, but I will not have you accosting our guests," Mr. Graven kept his voice stern and even. "I didn't do anything wrong," April said. "You slapped one of the resort's most honored guests. You will go up to him and you will apologize." "I will not. The man is a pig!" April said louder than she meant to. Mr. Graven pulled back his hand and aware of the crowd stopped himself. He lowered his voice and leaned in closer to April. "You are fired, do you understand? You will go to your cabin and pack your belongings. I expect to see you gone from here within the hour." April could not say anything else. She turned and ran down the hall as tears began to stream from her eyes, burning her cheeks in her shame and embarrassment.

Billionaire Nigel To The Rescue

Billionaire Nigel Conroy knew two things very well. Henry Worthington was a misogynist and a womanizer and the staff of Stuart would happily kiss the ground that he walked on. He was certain that Worthington could have murdered the poor girl and the staff supervisor would still have found a way to claim she had fallen upon his knife or gun herself. He also had a very good idea of who the girl was. His face was familiar, one he knew he had seen recently on the news. If he was right, she had been through enough. Being fired in front of all of the guests here was the last thing she needed. As the crowd began to slowly disperse, he took hold of the arm of another staff, a cute young woman with short blonde hair. "I'm sorry, but I wanted to ask you something before you had a chance to go away," Nigel said, releasing her. "It's alright sir," the young woman said. "How can I help you?" "The girl that just ran down the hall, what was her name?" The young woman narrowed her eyes, and Nigel did not blame her. He sensed protectiveness and found himself very much liking this young woman. "I don't mean any harm, but she didn't deserve what happened, and I think you know it. I'm pretty sure I've seen you here for a few seasons, so I think you know what really happened. I just want to make sure she'll be okay." The young woman continued to eye him warily. Nigel did his best to project his sincerity and she finally relaxed. "April Edwards. I can take you to see her. We share the same cabin." Nigel nodded his head. "Thank you. If anyone says anything, just tell them I pulled you aside to help me with an errand. I'll vouch for you, I promise." The young woman did not say anything else. She simply turned and Nigel understood he was expected to follow her. She led him through a side door of the main estate house.

The morning rain was now stopped, and the humidity of the afternoon was quickly setting in. She kept a brisk pace as she led him to the servant's cabins and to what he presumed to be her own. Nigel stepped into a small living area with a couch, chair, television, and three doors. The young woman turned to the left door and knocked gently. "April sweetie, it's Leah." "Please go away, Leah. I don't want to talk to anyone," April's muffled voice came through the door, thick with her tears. Leah looked back at Nigel but he nodded, waving his hand to urge her to continue. "April, there's a man here to see you," Leah said. The door swung open and April appeared, her face streaked with tears and fire in her eyes. Nigel felt a great deal of respect for her suddenly and felt very badly for anyone that earned that ire. He thought she could have a fiery temper, one she might not even be aware of. "I'll gouge out that bastard's eyes if it's him," April said before her eyes had a chance to survey the room. When they fell on Nigel, some of the fire pulled back, though he noticed it did not withdraw completely. "Who is that?" "He's one of the guests," Leah said. "He wanted to make sure you were okay." April stood there and studied Nigel before turning back to her friend. "Tell him I'll be fine." "Can I speak to you for a few minutes?" Nigel took a step forward. Leah looked from Nigel to April, and he could see the helplessness in her eyes. She had duties to attend to and could not be playing referee between them. April sighed and placed a hand on Leah's shoulder. "It's fine. You get back up before you get into trouble too." Leah hesitated, looked between the two of them again. She finally nodded. "You find me before you go, okay?" "I will. Thank you."

April gave Leah a hug. She released her and Leah walked past Nigel, giving him a careful look that he read very well. April had a bad enough day, and he did not need to make it worse. As Leah walked out of the cabin, Nigel turned his attention to the young woman before him as she stepped out of her room. She wore only the simple black dress common to all of the staff. The white apron had been discarded somewhere, either in her room or thrown aside as she fled the shameful scene. "You have a good friend. Have the two of you known each other a long time?" Nigel was curious about this young woman. The media had painted her as the aloof princess of a sinister financial king, carefully keeping herself out of the direct light of the media. He was not seeing that here. He was seeing something vastly different. "Just a few days. Leah is a real gem, though." April tilted her head to one side. "What are you doing here?" Nigel gave a small laugh. "You're not going to ask who I am?" April shook her head. "I know who you are. Your face shows up in almost every magazine, usually some story about a broken-hearted girl or a large playboy party." Nigel brought his hand up to his chest and feigned injury. "You wound me. But that's fair enough. I won't lie. I know who you are too." April frowned deeply. "Here to gloat then?" A sharp pain stabbed through Nigel's chest and he was surprised to feel it. He was not sure why he felt so much sympathy for this young woman. She was attractive. Her dark hair and bright, blue eyes would be enough to captivate any man. Something else had drawn him in, however. He just wished that he could put his finger on what it was. "No," Nigel said simply. "I really did want to make sure you were okay. Do you know what you're going to do?" April shook her head. "I can't go back down to New York. My face is still all over the television. I guess I get to hope that the few days of pay I have here is enough to fly me out to Los Angeles." "You don't have anyone that can help you out?" Nigel felt very badly for her now. He knew from the news reports that her father's assets had all been seized. He never imagined that it would leave her destitute. He wondered if anyone had bothered to care about that. "I talked to my mother. She's working as a waitress and trying to get into acting. She barely has enough money to pay her bills." April paused. "Why am I telling you this?"

A Surprising Invitation

Nigel was glad to see that at least both of them were behaving in ways they did not understand. She had an excuse. She was under duress. He had no idea what his excuse was, but he knew he would not be able to stop himself now. "Would you like to spend the rest of the week here with me, as my guest?" Nigel asked. April's look of shock made him smile. "What?" Nigel took in a deep breath and let it out. "I'm not sure why your supervisor was so hard on you, but I'm sure that you did not have it coming. A few broken cups are not worth risking a sexual harassment lawsuit. You don't have anywhere else to go right now. So, take a few days to figure it out. Maybe you and your mother will be able to work out something. In the meantime, enjoy the resort as a guest where your old boss can't touch you. As for Mr. Worthington, have the best revenge you can have on him." April crossed her arms. "What's that?" "Show him that it had no ill effect on you. Show him that you're over it and moved on. People who do things like that thrive on knowing the chaos they've caused." Nigel watched April carefully as she considered his proposal. She was wary, and he did not blame her. He knew how quickly people in his own circles could turn if they sensed weakness or unattractive controversy. He did not expect that people in hers would be any different. She finally uncrossed her arms and gave him a square look, setting her shoulders even. "What's the catch?" Nigel shook his head. "No catch. You'll have to stay with me, but I have one of the luxury cabins, so you'll have your own room. No expectations, except that you'll accompany me and keep me company. That's all." April continued to study him carefully. Finally, her stance relaxed. "Okay. I'll accept your invitation." Nigel nodded. "Good. Do you have street clothes?" April laughed. "Nothing worthy of a place like this." "Then I'll add one more caveat to this deal. Allow me to take you into town for a shopping trip." April nodded. Nigel sat down to wait for her to gather her things. This was a quaint and small cabin. He wondered if she had a chance to see the luxury guest cabins yet, and what she would make of them.

 April held her shopping bags in her hand as she followed Nigel up the walkway to the large cabin. Large picture windows dominated the façade, glowing through their translucent white shades. He carried her suitcase and occasionally made as though to be bearing too heavy of a weight. She could only laugh at that. Nigel Conroy the man was nothing like the man in so many magazine articles that she and her sorority sisters would read. She thought he could have his arrogant side, and occasionally as he took her through the shops in town, she saw it, typically, when he put down a dress or outfit because he felt the price tag was too low. Mostly, he was normal, if somewhat impulsive in taking her on as his guest. He opened the door to the cabin and held it for her to walk in. It opened immediately to the main room, open with a vaulted ceiling. A large fireplace dominated it with a couch and two oversized chairs set in front of it. A wide high definition television hung above the fireplace and a full entertainment system sat to the left side. Along the left wall stood a bar and to her right, the room opened to a dining room and a kitchen.

April wondered if it saw use at all and wondered at its inclusion. A stairway led up in front of her, dividing the mysterious kitchen from the rest of the downstairs. Nigel closed the door behind them and led her up the stairs. To her right, another large living area was set up with balcony rails so that it looked down below them. Beyond it was a hall with three doors. Nigel guided her to one and invited her to set down her things. A double bed sat in this room and an elegant dresser. She set her bags down beside the door as Nigel set her suitcase down by the dresser. "There's a bathroom right across the hall from you. If you don't like this bed, you can try the one in the room next to you. My room is at the end of the hall. I don't know if you do your own laundry. If you do, the French doors in the hall have a small washer and dryer behind them. You can also set your laundry in the bins outside for staff to pick up. It's your choice, but I do my own laundry." April blinked her eyes. "You do your own laundry?" She tried to imagine this man measuring out detergent and could not imagine it. "My housekeeper at home taught me after I ruined my own clothes at another resort. I've had bad luck with staff losing my things." April wondered if his items were lost or taken.

Most of the staff here were honest and hardworking, but she supposed that anyone could be tempted to take something that belonged to someone famous. "I suppose you cook too." Nigel shook his head. "No, that's never a pretty sight. I hoped you did, actually." April laughed and shook her head. "My cooking is part of our sorority's hazing ritual." She watched as he gave her a dubious look, tilting his head to one side. "I'm serious. I once boiled the coating out of a pan." Nigel leaned against the doorframe, his look becoming quickly serious and contemplative. "It's not fair, you know." I know. I have to be more careful with pots." April wanted the levity. The look in his eyes unsettled her. "I'm serious. It's fine that the Feds want to make sure your father pays back the money that he's taken. That's good. They can't take away his ability to care for the people he's responsible for. That punishes you for something you didn't do." April swallowed hard. She did not like the look in Nigel's eyes right now. It made her want to probe and want to understand the depth of empathy that he had at this moment. She did not want to do that. He was being nice to do this for her, but she did not want to complicate things any more than they were already complicated for her. "Right," Nigel pushed himself from the doorframe. "You've had a busy day, so I'll let you rest. I'll wake you up in the morning and we can go and enjoy brunch and some horseback riding if you like." "Horseback riding would be nice," April said. "Thank you again." Nigel smiled as he turned to the hall. "Thank you for accepting my invitation."

The young boy stood in front of the blazing fire, his eyes picking up the orange flames, reflecting them back to the world. Tears streamed down his soot-covered face and when he coughed, he sounded congested and full of smoke. Inside, in the flames, was everything he ever knew and understood to be love, compassion, and order. He could not understand what was happening, or why Nana uttered apologies as she tried to clean the soot from his face. April sat up in bed and took in a deep breath. Vivid dreams did not come on often, but when they did, they always left her feeling strange, as though she were coming back into her own body. It was, she thought, the effect of her mind moving from its dream reality back into the real world. The dream bothered her, and as her day played back in her mind and she remembered where she was, she understood why. She had found the story by chance. Her ex-boyfriend had a playboy magazine sitting on his bed, and she flipped through to the life story of Nigel Conroy, as promised on the cover, while he played on his game console. When Nigel was five years old, his mother had set fire to their home. She had drugged her husband and her son's nanny. She spread kerosene through the house, then over herself and her husband, lighting the both of them on fire. As the fire spread, Nigel's cries somehow managed to wake the groggy nanny, who stumbled out of the inferno, holding the crying child. The image in her dream was an image from the magazine article, a picture that had been taken of the boy as he stood watching the inferno that had been his home. He said in the interview for the article that he did not really remember the day, but it still influenced his life. His mother suffered from mental illness, untreated because both her family and his father had considered the idea of mental illness to be shameful, something that others faced, not them. Nigel had inherited his father's fortune, and when he was old enough to decide a direction for it, created a foundation to encourage the treatment and de-stigmatization of mental illness. How could she have forgotten such a terrible, tragic story? April put her head in her hands and began crying.

April followed Nigel up to the main estate house, where brunch waited for them. She wondered what Mr. Graven would make of her being there, or Leah for that matter. She thought about Chloe, who had gotten her the job. She hoped that Chloe was not told about what had happened. She hated to think that she would be made to regret helping her. Brunch was a pleasant affair, full of conversation. They sat at a large table with other resort guests and engaged in polite conversation. A few of the people at her table knew who April was, but none of them seemed to think her situation warranted more than a passing acknowledgment. She was happy about that. She noticed a glare from Mr. Graven. When he attempted to come to the table, Nigel rose and pulled him aside quickly. April did not know what was said exactly, only that it began with, "before you embarrass yourself." After brunch, they followed the other guests out to the veranda. There was no rain today, and the early afternoon was quickly growing warm. April followed Nigel through the crowd of people as he walked in the direction of the stables.

Horsing Around In The Stables

Mr. Worthington backed up, separating her from Nigel and almost causing April to run into him. He turned, startled, and gave her a kindly smile. "My apologies miss. My son was just clowning around as boys are want to do." "That's okay, Mr. Worthington," April said carefully. Mr. Worthington blinked his eyes and gave April a broader smile. "Well, I'm afraid you have me at a loss. You know me, but I don't know you." April smiled, feeling strange and light. After the huge scene the day before, he did not even recognize her face. She supposed that in the world Mr. Worthington inhabited, it was impossible that a woman who was a servant the day before could be a guest today. She supposed he had never seen Cinderella. "I'm afraid I'll have to leave it that way," April said. She glided past Mr. Worthington before he could stay anything else. Nigel had stopped and turned. He was now waiting on her, his look quickly became confused as she walked up to him. "What happened?" he asked. "I just bumped into Mr. Worthington," April said and decided to laugh. "He didn't even recognize me." Nigel blinked his eyes and tilted his head. April continued on to the steps that led down from the veranda. The stables were ahead, and she wanted to smell the fresh hay and the horses. Mr. Worthington did not think enough of the day to even realize she and the servant he tried to molest were the same people. If he could not be bothered, she supposed she did not need to either. The thought of putting the incident behind her lightened her step. After weeks of being remembered, a single moment of being forgotten was bliss.

Nigel's horse bucked and he pulled up on the reigns to gain control again, watching the young woman who laughed, carefree on the back of her own. She pulled up on the reigns and turned her horse so that she could twist in her saddle to look at him. This time yesterday, she was in tears. Now, she could have been a completely different person.

Nigel supposed in a way, she was. All she needed was a glass slipper and they could have been a prince and princess in a fairy tale. "You shouldn't look so serious," April said. "Horseback riding is supposed to be fun." "There's fun, and then there's slapping my horse's rump and startling him," Nigel said, but he found her smile to be infectious. April shrugged her shoulders. "You were riding like an old man. I just wanted to see if you really knew how to ride." Nigel took in a breath and nodded his head, recognizing the challenge. "I know how to ride, my dear. I took my first lesson at ten years old." "Seven," April gave him a smug look. "I still have you on years riding," Nigel said. He was only about six years older than April was, but his pride was wounded now. They continued their ride along the forest trail and up the mountain. It was beautiful here, and being out here among the natural beauty seemed to have a positive effect on April.

Nigel was not sure that he understood why her encounter with Mr. Worthington had left her in such a good mood, but it was nice to see that the forest around them was keeping it in place. They reached the water trough for the horses and dismounted, tying their reigns off on the poles there so the horses could drink and relax. This stop in the ride was along the ridge of the mountain that the horse trail wound. It offered a nice view of the valley and the estate below, and Nigel was happy to see that few others were taking advantage of the stables today. Most were heading out to the cricket grounds or down to the lake. Nigel turned to look at April and saw that she was watching him. The look in her eyes was deep and sympathetic. He wondered about it but was not sure what to ask her. Perhaps she was feeling bad about spooking his horse. "This is really nice," April said. She turned and looked back over the valley below them. "I really do appreciate you doing this for me." Nigel stepped up to her and took her hand in his. She did not pull away, and he held it tighter. As they looked over the valley, she talked about horseback riding in the boroughs outside of New York City and spending her entire weekend learning how to care for the horses. It was, she admitted to him, the only chore she ever learned to do, and one that she always loved. With her face in profile to him, Nigel could see that she was deeper in her thoughts than her words expressed. Was she remembering the good times with her father and mother, or was it just her father? He realized he had no idea how long her mother had been in Los Angeles. It could have been weeks or years. He had the feeling from how she had talked about her prospects of getting there that the two of them were not very close. April turned to face him, and Nigel found himself caught by her eyes. They were deep and contemplative while bright, catching the sky above them. Nigel brought his hand up to her face, cupping her cheek. He did not think about what he was doing. He simply leaned forward to kiss her.

Nigel's kiss was soft and careful, and it moved through April's body quickly, drawing her free hand up to his shoulders. Between her legs, she felt warm and alive. Nigel released her hand and moved his arm around her body, pressing her body closer to him. She could feel him hard against her and her own desire flared, surprising, and delighting her. He broke away and looked down into her eyes. April wanted his kiss again, and with a flush realized that she wanted more. She imagined their bodies entwined together here along the mountain ridge, where other riders could come upon them at any moment. The idea of it caused tingling and warmth between her legs. She reached up to kiss him again, finding him responsive and welcoming. Nigel brought his hand down from her face to her breast and cupped it gently. April wrapped her arms around his neck, running her fingers through Nigel's brown hair and lacing it through her fingers. He squeezed her breast and held her firmly against him. April wanted him. She wanted to feel his hands caress her body, to feel him deep inside her. Her body ached and screamed its want, and as the pounding of hooves came up the mountain trail, she could not pull away from him. They broke their kiss as another pair of riders came up to the trough. April flushed again and looked from Nigel to the newcomers. "That must be some view," the woman said as she dismounted her horse. She tied it off next to Nigel's own and looked at her partner. "Do you think we can take a look over the ridge too?" April stifled her laugh and took Nigel's hand, guiding him back to the horses. As they untied theirs from the trough, the new couple moved over to the ridge, sitting on the stone bench. April mounted her horse and waited for Nigel to join her. She considered heading back, but she wanted to push up the mountain. Yes, she wanted Nigel, and she thought if she told him she wanted to go back to his cabin now that he would. She also understood that part of that want came from moments like this, riding together and enjoying each other's company. She could let it build. They continued up the mountain trail, passing the new couple as the man put his arm around his companion. April supposed that the view really was romantic. She hoped there would be other such views on their way up.

They rode for another hour, and April could feel the heat of the day working into her body. A stream snaked along the slope of the mountain, coming close to the trail and skirting away from time to time. She thought about the hour, and how nice it would be to have a shower before they went up to the estate house for dinner. When she made the suggestion to Nigel that they head back, he was reluctant at first, until she mentioned showers. The look in his eye brought a new tingle between April's thighs. As they made their way back down the mountain, they passed the couple that had come up to the water trough. They exchanged waves and continued on, stopping only briefly at the trough to allow the horses to get water. April's mind kept turning to the shower waiting for them, and she did not want to stop any longer than necessary. She thought of water on her skin and Nigel caressing her body and grew impatient to be back. When they made it back down to the stables, the hands there took the horses from them, removing their tack and rubbing them down gently. They made their way across the estate grounds to the guest cabins, and April looked at Nigel. She could tell that he had something on his mind, and she wanted to be through it before they reached the cabin. "Is something the matter?" April asked. She could not think of any other way to get the conversation started. Nigel looked at her and gave her a gentle smile. "It was a beautiful ride, but I'm afraid I was a bit," he paused and looked up to find the words he needed, "presumptuous." April took in a deep breath and nodded her head. Oh, to get him to see how much she wanted that kiss. She did not want to come across as someone easy, or who was trying to get something from him, but she knew exactly what she wanted from the rest of her evening. "I told you I wasn't going to make any demands, and here I am crossing that line." Nigel placed his hands in his pockets. "It's not fair to you." April twisted up her lips in thought and nodded again. "It's not." When he snapped his head to her, she gave him a smile. "Well, it wouldn't be if I weren't receptive to it." Nigel narrowed his eyes and gave her a smile. He took her hand and picked up his pace.

The Billionaire's Desire

When they reached his cabin, he opened the door and she walked inside. When he closed the door behind them, his arms were around her body, pulling her back against him. April sighed and eased her stance so that she could feel his hardness pressing against her. "I want you so badly I can taste it," Nigel whispered into her ear. He nibbled the lobe gently. April turned around in his arms and brought her hands up to his shoulders. He pulled her tighter against him and April rose up to kiss him again. His tongue moved between her lips and danced with hers. She could taste his desire in his breath and wanted to drown in it. She brought her hands around to the collar of his shirt and slowly worked her way down his buttons. When he broke the kiss, Nigel lifted April's shirt above her head, discarding it to the side and shedding his own. He moved his hands down to her waist and unbuttoned her shorts, pushing them down her body. He started to kneel, and a panic-filled April. "I'm sweaty from the ride," April said. She wanted what his kneeling offered, but she wanted it to be perfect. Nigel stood. "Then let's have that shower." He pushed down her shorts and underwear in one motion. April slipped out of her shoes and her clothing, releasing the catch of her bra behind her back and dropping that as well. She was naked before

Nigel, and as his eyes took in her body, she shuddered, nervous. Would he find her pleasing? "You are beautiful." Nigel placed his hands at her waist and pulled her to him again. He kissed her deeply and then released her, gesturing her to walk up the stairs. He guided her back to his bedroom with its oversized king bed dominating the room, and then to the bathroom beyond. A large garden tub stood at one end of the bathroom. Next to it was a double-size shower with stone tiling. April stepped up to it and twisted the knobs on either side to start the water.

Nigel stepped up behind her and she could feel him, naked now, pressing against her. She stepped into the shower and he followed. Nigel took a large sponge and poured soap on it, lathering it in the stream of water that sprinkled over them. He brought it to April's body and caressed, leaving the soapy lather behind to be quickly washed away by the water. He moved along her chest, her arms, and her torso before moving down between and down her legs. When he finished, his lips were there, at her sex taking it in. April gasped and pressed her hands to the wall to support herself. His mouth was magic there, drawing her desire out of her and building it into a wave to crash over her body. She shivered as her body counted every bead of water that struck her. When he stood, April took the sponge from him, lathering it again, and running it across his shoulders, down his torso, and up his back. She brought it down to clean his manhood carefully and knelt, kissing what was now clean and hard softly before washing his legs, stroking down and then up along them gently. When she was through, she wanted to take him into her mouth, but he took hold of her arms and pulled her up. He kissed her and brought her leg up, pressing himself between her thighs.

She welcomed the feel of him hard and firm as he penetrated her. April wanted to feel him deeper, and when he brought her other leg up, she wrapped them around his body. He held her thighs and thrust deeper into her and she felt alive and desirous. She kissed him passionately as he pressed her against the wall, seeking the depth of her, joining with her in their shared passion. When he pulsed into her, April took hold of his hair, gripping it between her fingers, reveling as he pushed still deeper into her. When he was spent, he lowered her legs gently. April found them wobbly and weak, and stood under the warmth of the water, letting it pour energy back into them. Nigel kissed her again and pulled away, smiling as he dipped his head under the stream of water to wash his hair. "I like showers," April said. She brought her own head under the showerhead and hoped that the water would mask her embarrassment over saying something so silly. Nigel looked at her. "They can be very nice when the company is." A playfulness moved through April and she tilted her head to one side as she reached for the shampoo. "I tried to be very nice and you stopped me." Nigel laughed. "I didn't think that good girls were supposed to do that." April's mind turned and spun at his teasing. "I'm in a shower with a man I just met yesterday. How good of a girl can I be?" April's breath caught at the look in Nigel's eyes. It was both dark and desirous, and empathetic and sincere. She had no way to respond to it, and no word for the feeling it drew up inside her. She wanted to throw her arms around him and run away screaming at the same time.

Overcome by her fear and desire, she could only stand there, her hands at her head, ready to massage shampoo into her scalp. "You can be as good as you want to be," Nigel said. He brought shampoo up to his own head and closed his eyes as he worked it through his hair. April swallowed hard and washed her own as well. When he opened his eyes again, the depth of emotion had passed. April suppressed a shiver and wondered once again at this man. He was a playboy. This week and this affair were one of many he had, one of many that he would have. Some small part of her mind tried to challenge that, and April quashed it quickly as she rinsed her hair and turned off her side of the shower. This was just an affair, just like any other Nigel Conroy had. He was taking a young woman he saw in distress and helping her through it the only way he knew how to. She bore him no ill will for that. In fact, April thought the world could use a few more Nigels.

The dining hall was lit brightly tonight, and a string quartet played Vivaldi as guests entered. Nigel led April to a table for two and they sat down, waiting patiently for a server to come by. Evening meals were meant to be more intimate, but the menu was still a general fare for all guests, a choice of steak, chicken, or fish, with either rice or potatoes and summer vegetables. April decided that she would have the fish and rice while Nigel ordered a steak and requested a bottle of wine to be brought out to them. April spotted Leah among the servers and gave her a small wave. She did not want to embarrass Nigel, and while she thought he would understand her wanting to say hello to her friend, she knew that the other guests would consider the gesture to be gauche at best. Leah gave her a small and excited wave, looking from April to Nigel and back. She mouthed, "wow" as she poured water for another table, and moved to another. April gave an innocent shrug and smiled. Nigel looked over his shoulder and back to April, smiling. "I think you've inspired new dreams in the female staff." April laughed. "If only it were that easy for romance." She paused and thought about her last two days. "I'm not even sure how this happened." Nigel reached under the table and brushed April's knee lightly. She could see he wanted to say something, but before he could, a man walked up to the table. Nigel withdrew his hand casually and looked up at the newcomer. It took April a moment to register who the man was, and panic filled her. This was Chloe's father, and she could imagine the story told to him, and the reprimand her friend received. April had never met Michael Stuart when she was hired on, she only worked with Mr. Graven, but she understood him to be a shrewd and clever businessman. "Mr. Conroy, it is always a pleasure to have you here at the Estate." Mr. Stuart turned his attention to April and gave her a broad smile. "Ms. Edwards, it is good to see that you're enjoying your stay with Mr. Conroy. My daughter sends her regards."

April relaxed at the tone in Mr. Stuart's voice. Whatever story had gotten to his ears, it was either not believed, or countered, perhaps by Chloe herself. April made a note to herself. If she could not find her friend this summer, she would do so during the school year – assuming she was able to get back down to New York City to attend the university. "Thank you. Please tell Chloe I said hello." Mr. Stuart nodded his head. "I will. She's enjoying a nice trip in Europe right now. She's spending the summer studying there as part of a fellowship. I will be sure to let her know when I talk to her. The both of you enjoy your evening." He walked away from the table and over to another. April looked to Nigel to see him smiling wisely. "What?" she asked. "You looked like a deer caught in headlights for a moment there," Nigel said. "The whole reason that I had a job here is that Chloe convinced her father to hire me. I was afraid that the worst of what happened reached him." Nigel shook his head. The server brought their wine and poured a glass for each of them. When she left, leaving the bottle on the table between them, Nigel spoke. "I doubt anyone would have dared to say anything to him. The whole situation would have had him asking too many questions and probably getting other people not you fired. He probably wouldn't do anything to Worthington, though he should, but there are limits to what even Mr. Stuart can do." April sipped her wine. She had not thought about just how precarious of a position that Mr. Graven really was in with how he had fired her and why. It occurred to her that she could file a complaint, but she realized she did not want to.

The Philanthropic Playboy

Mr. Graven seemed to really care about his staff. His attitude toward her did not mask that. She doubted the scene would have played out quite the same way if it had been anyone else. The situation may have been hushed. The girl may even have been reassigned to other duties while Mr. Worthington was here. She thought that other things aggravated the situation, and while it was not right for Mr. Graven to hold her accountable for her father's actions; it was not worth him losing his job over. "You're a good person," Nigel said. April blushed, wondering if he read her mind, or if he just understood the situation itself. "Thank you." "I mean it, you are." Nigel sipped his wine. "Anyway, I'm glad that you accepted my invitation." "I am too." They enjoyed their dinner together, using the time to chat and get to know each other a little better. That tiny voice April's head tried to ask her if that was the kind of conversation that playboys engaged in, and she refused to answer. Her life was complicated, very complicated. She did not need to complicate someone else's as well. After dinner, they wandered the estate house, seeing what festivities were taking place tonight. A company was holding an important shareholder meeting in one of the conference rooms. Both of them thought that was too boring to enjoy. Staff cleared the dining hall and the string quartet continued playing music. Guests who were not taking part in the shareholder meeting or any of the other smaller events filled up the dining hall, dancing to baroque music and enjoying the evening on the veranda. April and Nigel joined in this. Nigel showed April a few simple steps for ballroom dancing, and they moved together to the music. With his arm around her waist, leading her in steps, April felt her desire swell up through her body again. She wanted to kiss him and knew that would not be proper here. They spotted the couple from the trail and exchanged smiles.

As they danced past, April caught a snippet of their conversation and realized they were enjoying their anniversary here together. "This is a magical place," April said as Nigel guided her off the dancefloor and over to a table where drinks were set out for guests. "Oh?" Nigel handed her a glass of punch and looked at her curiously. "The couple on the trail today, they're enjoying their anniversary here." Nigel glanced out to the floor. "Is that so?" "Apparently. I wonder how many other people are here for special occasions." Nigel paused as he brought his glass to his lips and considered the people out on the dance floor. "I've never thought about it. I always just come up here and enjoy the mountains and the lake. I don't really think about what is going on with the rest of the guests unless I know them personally." "I wonder about people sometimes," April said. "When I was a child, I would watch people on the street and wonder where they were going to and coming from. When we would be in a restaurant, I would imagine what conversations people were having at other tables. I always found my life to be easy and boring, so it was a fun way to make things interesting." "Oh, for things to be easy and boring." April looked and saw Nigel's eyes turn dark with thought again. She supposed that for him, a boring life would have been ideal. She could not imagine what it would have been like for him. Did he have grandparents battle for custody of him, or did servants and lawyers raise him? He did not talk about that in the Playboy interview. April found herself curious again and wondered if she would have the chance to explore that deep into him.

They danced for a few more songs before walking out onto the veranda and back up to Nigel's cabin. They held hands as they walked, taking in the view of the stars above them. April concentrated on trying to remember the names of any of the stars and constellations she saw and was ashamed that she could not. She should know them. She had learned about them in high school. She never applied herself, and that knowledge drove home her precarious situation. She always assumed that he father's money would be there to take care of her. She would just move from that security to the security of a man. Now, that option was not open to her. She was not marriageable material. She was fine for a fling, but she did not want to live her life being the naughty fling of rich men. She was going to have to decide on a direction for herself. She realized that depending on her mother was not the answer either. She was an adult. It was time that she acted it, and took on the responsibilities that brought. Nigel let her into the cabin and followed her inside. He walked to the fireplace and turned on the gas starter. The logs, April realized, were only for show, to create a simulated fireplace. It was still beautiful, however, and she found herself pushing aside her thoughts and worries for another day. She walked over to the couch and sat down. Nigel joined her and when he leaned close to her, April welcomed his kiss and his arms around her waist. She thought of making love to him in front of the fireplace and her excitement grew. He broke the kiss and brought his hand up to April's cheek. She looked into Nigel's eyes and wondered at what thoughts were behind them. His eyes still looked contemplative and serious. "I want you to stay with me," Nigel said. April smiled. "I can sleep in your room if you'd like." She knew that was not what he meant, even as she said the words. She did not want to have the conversation that was coming.

She realized that she had been running from it since their shower today and she thought she understood why now. "That will be nice, but that's not what I mean," Nigel said. April put her finger on his lips. He took her hand and kissed the back of it, bringing it back down to her lap. "It is not fair," he said. "You're going through something you should not have to go through. Nothing that happened is your fault, but you're suffering for it." "Lots of people suffer for things that aren't their fault." April suspected that Nigel suffered a lot. What was it actually like, growing up the son of a woman who killed herself and her husband? How many years did he spend wondering if that would happen to him? Nigel let out a sigh. "They do. I would help every single one of them if I could. We can't. We can only help those we can." He paused and sat back."Do you know about what happened when I was a child?" April nodded her head. "I read an interview where you talked some about it." "The woman who took me out of the fire, she was my nanny. She was a kind woman. She was stern, and I grew up thinking she was mean sometimes. She took care of me. She did not have to stay with me. She could have let my family's lawyers find someone else. She was burned very badly in the fire. I lied when I told the interviewer I didn't remember the night very well. I did, but I didn't want to talk about it. She refused to let the paramedics treat her or take her to the hospital until she knew I was okay. She ended up being scarred very badly because of that, but it was the kind of woman she was. She stayed because I was the person she could help." April took in a deep breath and squeezed Nigel's hand tightly. "I want to help you. You were not working here because you wanted to. You were here because you had to be. No one should have to work like that. I don't want you to have to work like that."

April felt her heart filling and breaking at the same time. She cared about Nigel, more deeply and more quickly than she thought she would ever care about anyone. She could see herself easily falling in love with him, if she were not there already. She appreciated what he wanted to do, and she thought she understood what it meant to him. That did not mean she could just accept it. "Did you know I couldn't name a single constellation in the sky tonight?" April asked. Nigel gave a small laugh. "I think I know the Big Dipper and Little Dipper. Not everyone knows the constellations." "No, but people can point to the things they do know," April said. "I can't. My whole life I have depended on other people. I depended on my father to put me through school. I knew I just had to wait to get married and have another man to depend on for my livelihood. If it didn't work out, I would be able to get a nice alimony settlement and probably more money from Daddy again. "I can't do that anymore. It doesn't matter that it's not fair. If I go back to school, I can get a real degree. I can figure out what I want to do with my life and do it, and not have to depend on anyone else."Nigel brought his hand up to her cheek again. "It's a hard place, I know. The most important person in your life let you down, and depending on another person after that is scary. What happens if I let you down?" April felt her heart break. She did not want to look at Nigel that way, but he was right. That was exactly what she was scared of. It was more than that, though. She could not expect him to pick up where others left off in taking care of her. It was not just a matter of what he might do anymore. It was what she had to do. "You're such a wonderful person," April said. She leaned against the back cushion of the couch and let herself gaze into Nigel's eyes. "From most of the stories I've read about you, you're this carefree playboy who does philanthropy and just enjoys his money. You really are so much more than that. It's not that I think you would hurt me. I'm scared of it, but I know better. It's also what I have to do for me." Nigel leaned his head against the back cushion and looked at her, silent in whatever contemplation he was in. "I have no idea how I'm going to do this. A lot of people work their way through college. Some of them take student loans. I can do that too if I have to. If I talk to the financial counselors, they'll help me find a job and work out a schedule that I can pay for. I can always change schools if I need to. People do it every day. I'm no one special; I just thought I was for a long time." Nigel let out a deep breath. She could see understanding and acceptance in his eyes. "I could see you with a career. I think if you find something that you're passionate about, you could really put yourself into it and do something amazing," he said. "I would like to see that." April smiled. "Thank you." "Can I pay for school?" Nigel sat up again. April was stunned and unsure how to answer his question. He had turned this around somehow and she felt as though she had been flipped on her head. "Pay for school?" Nigel nodded. "I see the people who work their way through college. Sometimes they can pursue what they want. Sometimes they have to compromise. I want you to find and pursue whatever you want. I can pay for your school. You can stay on campus or with me, whichever you want. I won't pressure you there, though I would like to keep seeing you after this week."

April's mind was still trying to catch up to this strange change in their conversation. She tried to find words, and could not get anything to make sense from her mind to her mouth. "You can say yes," Nigel said. "I would really like that." April let out a laugh and sat up. She shook her head and looked down, trying to let her mind finish playing catch up. Nigel was serious about helping her. She did not think it was just some passing fancy of his. His understanding and his persistence told her how intent he was on this. She looked up and smiled at him. "Okay. But I get to pay you back for my school, even if I'm just donating it to your foundation. I appreciate it, but I want to be able to give something back to you." Nigel returned her smile and broadened it. "I can accept that. You will have to apply yourself, though. I fully expect you to find a career that you can follow through on." April moved closer to him on the couch. "I promise. I'll think about it this summer and decide." She paused before kissing him and pulled back. "What do I do during the summers?" Nigel put his arms around her waist and pulled her down to him. "I'm sure we can negotiate something." He kissed her. April welcomed his tongue through her lips. She thought again of making love to him in front of the fireplace and moved her hands up to unbutton his shirt. It was a good place to start.

The Job Search Begins

April loved being adored by Nigel. He knew how to calm her nerves and work through her age-related angsty moods. She went to college to get a degree so that she could forge a meaningful path in the world, not be someone's sugar baby. When Nigel was away on business, she decided to apply for a job. She didn't need the money, but she wanted to earn an income in case he ended their relationship. She knew that if she expressed her desire to find work, Nigel would disapprove of it and discourage her. She didn't want to work in retail or customer service, so she applied for a job as an assistant to the CEO of a steel company. She heard rumors about the billionaire steel magnate. Not only was he filthy rich, gorgeous, single, and wealthy, but he was also somewhat of a tyrant. To say he was rude and condescending would be an understatement.

"Ms. April Edwards?" a mature friendly-looking woman asked her and smiled at her.

"Yes, I'm April Edwards," she replied.

"Mr. Fairfield will be with you shortly. He's very busy today and almost had to cancel your interview, but he found your cover letter and resume intriguing and wanted to find out more about you as soon as possible."

"Oh goodness, that was fast! Mr. Fairfield just buzzed me on the intercom. He's ready to see you now. Please follow me." The woman was sharply dressed in a form-fitting black dress that was hardly appropriate for office wear, but it worked for her. The two women got into the elevator, where it took them up to the penthouse office. April had to stifle a gasp when she saw it. It was the most stunning space that she had ever seen. Even Nigel's office wasn't this grand. Thinking about Nigel made her feel sad because she felt deceitful. He wanted to take care of her and asked nothing in return. He was truly one in a million and she felt blessed that he walked into her life that day at the country club. April could just smell the old money in that penthouse office. Nigel was wealthy, but Fairfield had him beat. I was sure of that. The adrenaline rush she felt when entering the penthouse was almost too much for her. She had to focus on her breathing to avoid fainting.

"Ms. Edwards, it's certainly a pleasure to meet you. Please sit down."
"Good morning, Mr. Fairfield. The pleasure is all mine." Looking at his steel-blue eyes, wavy black hair, perfect teeth, and muscular build weakened her knees. He was dressed impeccably and smelled very expensive. My heart was racing, and for a split second, I wished that I wasn't with Nigel. It would make things easier. Nigel was distinguished-looking, kind, and responsible. Mr. Fairfield was the sexiest man I've seen in my life and he was surrounded by the most profound alpha bad boy aura that I've ever encountered. He was cordial, but there was an air of arrogance about it.

"What makes you think you're qualified to be my personal assistant, Ms. Edwards? Your resume is quite thin and lacking in the necessary experience. It states that you were a college student and then worked a summer job at a country club."

"Yes, my resume is a bit "thin," but I'm a fast learner and eager to do anything that's put in front of me," she said.

"I believe that I have met your father on a few occasions. We traveled in the same social circle once upon a time. How is the old man?"

April felt the anger and resentment rising up into her throat. She knew that Fairfield knew her father was arrested for running a Ponzi scheme, was in jail. and lost every penny of his fortune. "He's doing very well, thank you." She sensed that he took pity on her, but according to his reputation, he's ruthless and cares only about himself and his money. He's no Nigel, that's for sure.

"You're right in saying that I lack experience, but I graduated summa cum laude and was first in my class," said April, trying to prevent her throat from tightening as she spoke.

"Do you have a special person in your life, Ms. Edwards? A boyfriend or husband who takes care of your needs? All of your needs? I'm just curious as to why you would want to take on the job as my personal assistant. I demand a lot of time from my assistants and sometimes my needs are, shall we way, unconventional," he said in a low growling tone. "My business style is a little unusual and it's sometimes off-putting to novice assistants who haven't had any experience working with people such as myself," he explained.

April shot back, "Please forgive me if I don't answer your question. I don't feel my relationship status is relevant to the job I'm applying for, nor is it any of your business. Good day, Mr. Fairfield," she said with venom in her voice.

"Ms. Edwards, please don't go. I realize that I was being intrusive and rude by asking you those questions," he said. She noticed that his face was flushed and beads of perspiration were forming on his forehead. She questioned the sincerity of his tone and was irked that he didn't apologize, but she decided to stay and finish the interview. He was aggressive and he reeked of sex. Poor Nigel, she thought. I want to sleep with Fairfield so bad. I've never felt like this before about any man, Nigel included. Sure, Nigel is handsome, educated, and funny, but he lacks that bad boy quality that stirs my soul. I'm ambitious and by working as Mr. Fairfield's assistant, I know that I can prove myself in the corporate world. Staying with Nigel would be nice too, but with him, I'll never be able to challenge myself professionally. I don't want to settle for domestic mediocrity with a man who caters to my every whim.

I'm a go-getter and a bit of a rebel. I'm also horny as hell for my prospective new boss. With Nigel, I have everything that money can buy.

A gorgeous home, money, security, and love. I cherish my life, I really do, but strangely, I feel empty inside. Maybe it's because I came from money. Growing up, we lived in a huge house located in a gated community in one of the wealthiest neighborhoods in the nation. Money doesn't excite me. I needed it after my father got arrested and we lost everything. Nigel couldn't have stepped into my life at a better time. I don't know what I would have done had he not, but I'm young, curious, eager, and ambitious. I can be all those things with Fairfield. I can be a tigress instead of the demure kitten that Nigel makes me out to be.

Michael Fairfield was a smooth talker and he had a brilliant mind. Multiple personal assistants were in his employ, so why did he need to hire another one? Perhaps his personal needs were darker than I had anticipated. There was an unusual sweetness to his face that concealed the beast within him.

"You're different from the other girls I've interviewed for this position," he remarked.

"Girls, Mr. Fairfield?"

"Sorry, I meant applicants," he retorted.

"How am I different? Do you mean that in a complementary way? If you mean that the applicants were more experienced than I, then yes, I am different," she countered.

She sensed that he was getting charged up. If she didn't know any better, she'd swear that his pants were getting tighter in the crotch area too.

"Ms. Edwards, I'd like your opinion on something. I have a meeting with my board of directors next week to discuss a merger between my company and a rival steel corporation," he said.

"What would you like my opinion on?"

"Well, for starters, the president of the company is my ex-wife. She started the business with the money I gave her from our divorce settlement. She now wants to merge with my business, but I'm not sure if it's a good idea. I think that business-wise it might be lucrative, but I think her motives are more personal. I'd really like your input," he said.

"First of all, before I can offer an opinion, I'd have to ask if she's trying to reconcile with you. I mean, has she expressed a desire to get back together with you?" she asked. "There are lots of good reasons for corporate mergers, but trying to get back with your ex-husband isn't one of them," she explained.

"I'd like to offer the job, Ms. Edwards," he said.

"We spoke only briefly about my qualifications, goals, and work style," she replied. "How do you know that I'd be a good fit?" she asked.

"I have a feeling that you'd fit my needs like a glove, Ms. Edwards. In more ways than one," he moaned.

First Day On The Job

April accepted Michael's offer but after learning more about the position, she had her doubts. Not only did he require her to be his travel companion to Paris, Milan, London, and Asia, but he would also require her to pose as his girlfriend. The reason for her going back to work was to prove to herself and Nigel that she could pay her own way. She didn't want Nigel supporting her. She also feared that he would dump her, leaving her to fend for herself, with no money and no job skills. She wanted to work in a corporate environment to hone her management skills but working as Michael's personal assistant/fake girlfriend probably wouldn't add any credence to her resume. She could understand why he would need his personal assistant to accompany him on business trips, but for the life of her, she couldn't understand why she would be required to pose as his girlfriend. He could have any woman he wanted. In fact, everywhere he went, beautiful women threw themselves at him. He had a different woman every night of the week. What was it about April that he wanted? He offered her the job without knowing much about her. She should have known something was up the way he leered at her when she walked into his office.

"April, I need you to pick out a few dresses at the Amara Boutique for me. I'm giving them to a few close business associates who work in the fashion industry. Do you think you're up for the challenge?" he asked. "Yes, Sir, I'd be happy to. I don't know if I'm the right person for the job though. I'm not what you would call a "fashion plate," and I only own a couple of dresses, which are very conservative. I don't know much about couture or high fashion," she replied.

"That's quite alright. You don't need to know anything about fashion. I'll accompany you to the boutique and I'll choose the dresses. I do need you to try the dresses on, however. I want to get an idea of how they'll look. You know, how the fabric flows and everything." April almost walked out right then and there. This wasn't what she bargained for and never heard of a personal assistant's job description as having to try on dresses for their boss. She ended up going to the boutique with Michael, and to her surprise, she actually had a good time...for a while, at least. They laughed and joked around, but when it came time for her to try on their dress selections, she hesitated. "Mr. Fairfield, I don't really feel comfortable trying on these dresses for you. Isn't there any way that you can purchase the garments without me having to try them on? The store has a very liberal return policy. If your business associates don't like the dresses or if they don't fit, the boutique will refund the price of the dresses with no questions asked," she said. "I'm sorry, April, that's not possible. I need you to try on these dresses, and just so you are aware, this job duty is one that is required of all my personal assistants. If you're not comfortable with it, then I will have to retract my offer of employment. This is a mandatory job duty and must be fulfilled if you want to work for me," he said. "In addition, if I didn't make myself clear during your interview, you are also required to share my hotel room with me when we travel on business. It's true that I'm a wealthy businessman, however, money doesn't grow on trees, and the hotels I stay at are five-star hotels and are very expensive. Booking two rooms is too much of an expense and doesn't make sense to do so."

April was outraged. She had a loving and caring boyfriend at home. While she wanted to pay her own way by getting a job, she wasn't going to demean her relationship with Nigel by posing as this guy's girlfriend. That's bad enough, but having to stay in his hotel room with him on business trips was something that she wasn't willing to do. "I'm sorry, Sir. This job doesn't align with my beliefs, so I'm going to decline the offer. I wish we would have discussed the details earlier."

"You can't quit like this. I won't allow it. You see, you have more at stake here than you realize. Do you know who I am?"

Thanks, But No Thanks

What did he mean, "Do you know who I am?" April knew very well who he was. He was billionaire CEO, Michael Fairfield, who owned multiple companies in the United States and abroad. What else was there to know about him and why did he say that in such a cryptic tone? "Yes, Mr. Fairfield, I do know who you are and I respect you for everything that you have accomplished," she said. "No, April, I don't think you understand. It's true that I am Michael Fairfield, but I have more of a connection to you than you know. You see, I am Nigel Conroy's long-lost brother. I am also the executor of our family's empire, and therefore, I control all of the finances. Nigel knows that one of his family members has sole control of the corporation's finances, but it's a long-held secret who that family member is. It was our great-great grandfather's wish for the executor of the corporation to remain anonymous. I didn't realize that you were Nigel's girlfriend until I did some investigating when you applied for the job as my personal assistant. It was then that I decided I needed to have you comply with my unusual job requests."

To say that April was shocked would be an understatement. Even though he did some "investigating," how did he discover that she was Nigel's girlfriend? Did he have connections to the country club where she worked? For a moment, she even considered that he may have had connections to the person who touched her inappropriately at the country club and the one who got her fired. "I never really liked what

Nigel was all about," he said. "Everything always came easy for him. He had a great personality, went to the best schools, and was well-liked by everyone. Me? I had to struggle for everything. My father was a strict disciplinarian and never doled out compliments to his kids. The only child that got compliments and praise was Nigel. Those compliments built up his self-esteem, which helped him succeed in life. I was always the one who was put down. My father was always hard on me and seldom showed any pride when it came to my accomplishments. So you see, April, now, I have some control over my brother. I can control his girlfriend and if I choose to do so, I can make his girlfriend my girlfriend. Oh sure, you might not be my girlfriend in real life, but in the eyes of my business associates, you'd be mine, and that's enough for me."

"Mr. Fairfield, what difference does it make if your business associates think I'm your girlfriend?" He replied, "It makes a big difference. Most of the people I do business with, domestically and internationally, know that Nigel is my brother. Nigel has told them all about you. They know your name, what you look like, and where you're from. They even know that your father was arrested for his involvement in that Ponzi scheme. They respect Nigel. When they find out that you're now my girlfriend, they'll respect me."

April couldn't believe what she was hearing. She didn't care if Michael's business associates respected him or not. What he was doing to both me and Nigel was dirty. She didn't want any part of it, but nonetheless, she was intrigued. How did he concoct this elaborate scheme? He had to know that one day Nigel would find out. If he did find out, he would go to the board of directors and sing like a canary and tell them everything he knew. Had I known then what I know now, I would have never gotten involved with Nigel when I met him on that fateful day at the country club. But now that I do know him, I've decided that I want to keep him. If he wants to support me and take care of me like I'm his princess, then so be it. Who am I to want to go out and find a job. If taking care of me brings him pleasure, then it's pleasure he shall have.

"Thank you, Mr. Fairfield, for the most interesting job experience I've ever had. If I'm ever in need of a job as a dress modeler, I'll give you a call. In the meantime, stay true to the Conroy name, and be more like Nigel. Good, kind, and fair. In the long run, nice guys finish first."

keywords: billionaire romance, billionaire boss, billionaire bad boy, alpha billionaire, billionaire ceo, bad boy billionaire, billionaire hero, billionaire boyfriend, billionaire protector, billionaire banker, billionaire scandal, billionaire kisses, billionaire boys club, billionaire games, billionaire romance books, billionaire ebooks, steamy billionaire romance, dark billionaire romance, dark billionaire romance books, alpha billionaire club, the billionaire's secret, the billionaire's game, baby for the billionaire, the billionaire's secret baby, billioanaire romance books

www.ingramcontent.com/pod-product-compliance
Ingram Content Group UK Ltd.
Pitfield, Milton Keynes, MK11 3LW, UK
UKHW040843050326
11084UKWH00029B/957